Home to Me, Home to You

By Jennifer A. Ericsson ❧ Illustrated by Ashley Wolff

LITTLE, BROWN AND COMPANY

New York ❧ Boston

Little, Brown and Company

Time Warner Book Group
1271 Avenue of the Americas, New York, NY 10020
Visit our Web site at www.lb-kids.com

First Edition

Library of Congress Cataloging-in-Publication Data

Ericsson, Jennifer A.
 Home to me, home to you / by Jennifer A. Ericsson ; illustrated by Ashley
Wolff. — 1st ed.
    p. cm.
 Summary: A child at home and a mother flying back from a business trip
think of each other as they eagerly await their reunion.
  ISBN 0-316-60922-6
 [1. Mother and child — Fiction. 2. Separation (Psychology) — Fiction.] I.
Wolff, Ashley, ill. II. Title.
PZ7.E72584Ho 2005
[E] — dc22

                                                                2003020583

10 9 8 7 6 5 4 3 2 1

PHX

Printed in China

The illustrations for this book were done in Gouache on Arches Cover paper.
The text was set in ITC Stone Serif and Kidprint MT. The display type is Parango.

To Annie — you are "home" to me!

— J.A.E.

For Morgan Witham Berg
and her baby sister Riley
Ellen Berg.

—A.W.

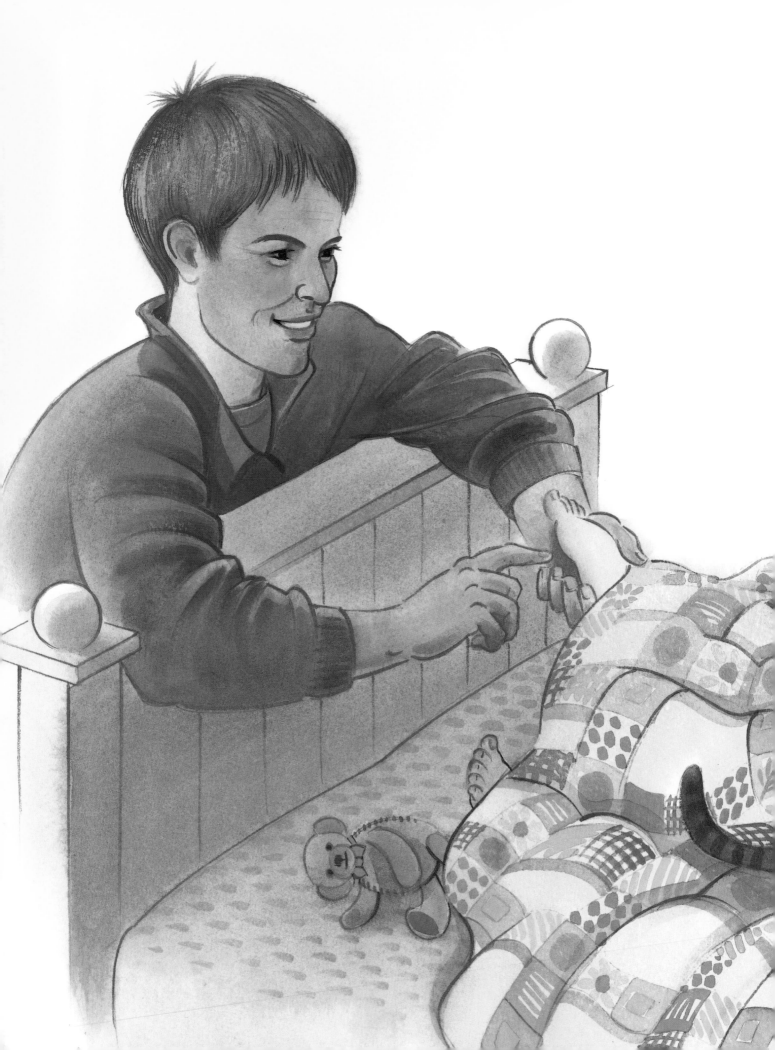

"Good Morning, Monkey," says Daddy.
"Do you remember what today is?"
I yawn and think. Then I'm wide awake.
"Today is the day Mommy comes home!"
I shout.

Home to me.

The hotel alarm goes off very early.
I pack my luggage and leave for the airport.
I haven't seen you or daddy all week,
but now I'm heading home.

Home to you.

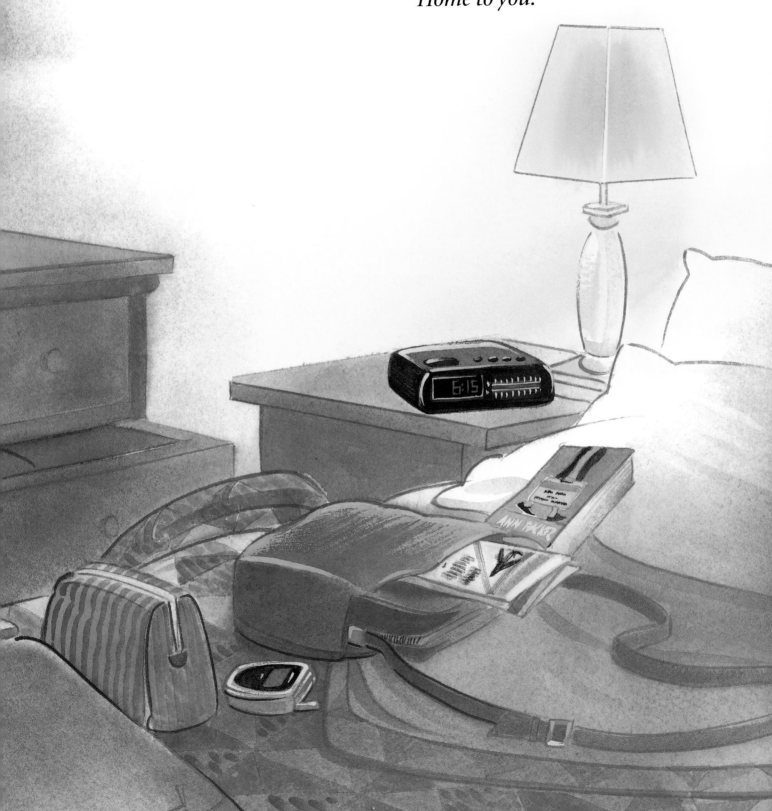

After breakfast, my playgroup comes over
and we set up my blocks.
We make a lot of tall buildings
and roads full of cars.
We make an airport too, and I fly
one of the planes high over our city.
"This is my mommy coming home," I say.

The plane takes off, and everything on the
ground shrinks to the size of your toys.
The skyscrapers and looping highways
get smaller and smaller.
I think about all the hard work I did on my trip,
and about how long it will take to get back home.

Daddy makes my favorite lunch.
He even peels my orange
and pulls it apart just the way I like it.
"Look under your plate," he says.
I peek and find a note from Mommy.
Hurry home, Mommy.

I stare out the window and think of the voice
message you left me at the hotel.
"Hi, Mommy, it's me. I miss you."
I played it over and over just to hear your voice.
But tonight I won't need it. Tonight I'll be home.

I take out paper and markers and stickers.
I'm going to decorate invitations for
my birthday party.
Mommy will be so proud of me!
I'll show them to her when she gets home.

I open my briefcase and try to get some work done.
There are lots of reports to read and letters to write.
The more I do now, the less I'll have to do when I get home.

I lie down for my nap with
all my favorite toys.
Daddy tucks me in.
I hear a plane fly across the sky.
Is that Mommy's plane?
Fly home, Mommy.

I tilt my seat back and shut my eyes.
I drift off to sleep to the plane's constant rumble.
I dream about you and Daddy.
I dream about coming home.

When I wake up, Daddy helps me make a fort
with a blanket and some chairs.
We crawl inside and break up chocolate cookies
into mugs of cold milk.
Then we eat them with a spoon.
"I wish Mommy was home," I say.

My plane lands at the first stop.
I'm only halfway home.
When I check on my flight, I find out it will be delayed.
I call you and Daddy to let you know
I'll be late getting home.

"Mommy is on the phone," calls Daddy.
"Do you want to say hi?"
I like hearing Mommy's voice,
but she sounds so far away.
"When will you be home?" I ask.

The plane takes off again.
The flight attendant brings a cold drink
and small packs of salty peanuts.
"My daughter loves these," I say.
I eat one pack but put the other in my purse to bring home.

Daddy and I make dinner together.
I set three places at the table.
"That one is for Mommy," I say.
"She'll probably be hungry when she gets home."

My plane lands at last.
I gather my coat and bags and leave the airport.
I sing along with the radio as I drive north, toward home.

After dinner, I get ready for my bath.
"Hop in the tub, Monkey," says Daddy.
I scrub all over so I'll be nice and clean
when Mommy comes home.

The sun sinks, spreading beautiful colors across the sky.
I run a brush through my hair and repack my briefcase.
We're getting close — close to home.

I snuggle on the couch with Daddy
and a pile of my books.
I hear a car pull into the driveway.
"Is that Mommy?" I ask. "Is she home?"

It is dark, but the lights are on inside the house.
I see you and Daddy standing at the window.
It is so good to be finally home.

Home to you.

I run to the door and pull it open.
Mommy drops her bags and grabs me in a giant hug.
"You're home, Mommy!"

Home to me.

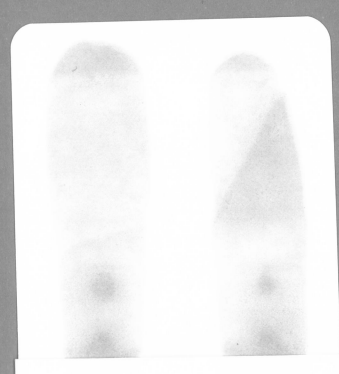